Ghost of the Great River Inn

Follett Publishing Company/Chicago

Weekly Reader Books presents

Ghost of the Great River Inn

LYNN HALL

Illustrated by Allen Davis

This book is a presentation of
Weekly Reader Books.

Weekly Reader Books offers
book clubs for children from
preschool through junior high school.
All quality hardcover books are selected by
a distinguished Weekly Reader Selection Board.

For further information write to:
Weekly Reader Books
1250 Fairwood Ave.
Columbus, Ohio 43216

Cover design by José Pacheco

Designed by Karen A. Yops

Library of Congress Cataloging in Publication Data

Hall, Lynn.
  Ghost of the Great River Inn.

  Summary: After seeing the ghost of a paymaster
murdered during the Civil War, two fourth grade friends
in Iowa make a startling discovery.
  [1. Ghost stories] I. Davis, Allen. II. Title.
PZ7.H1458Gh [Fic]   80–18585
ISBN 0–695–41465–8

Some Similar Books
by Lynn Hall

Chapter 1

"You kids hang on, back there. I don't want any broken heads." Sandy's father climbed into the pickup truck and slammed the door.

In the two forward corners of the truck bed Sandy West and Alan Trumbull braced themselves and got firm holds on the wooden framework of the truck's stock box. The engine roared. The metal floor beneath Alan's feet jolted forward. He hung on and grinned into the cold air that struck his face.

It was late on a Friday afternoon in March. An hour earlier the school bus had deposited Alan and Sandy at the Wests' farm lane, and the weekend Alan had been eagerly awaiting began. His parents had gone to Chicago for a pharmacists' convention and had let him choose the friend he wanted to stay with while they were gone. His choice was Sandy.

"But she's a girl," his other friends had hooted. Even his parents had been surprised by his choice. But Alan was stubborn about some things. He liked Sandy. They were in the same fourth grade room in McGregor Consolidated School. Gradually, through the school year, their friendship had grown, despite the differences of boy-girl and town-country.

Over the truck noise and the wind Alan yelled, "Where are we going? I thought your dad said we were going to get hay for the horses."

They had bumped the length of the farm lane and were turning onto the road, leaving the farm.

"We are," Sandy yelled back. "We're going over to the stone barn. It's across the road and down a ways. There, you can see it, over there."

She waved and Alan looked. To his right lay a broad, flat half-circle field, tawny and gray with hay stubble and old snow. On the back rim of the field stood a two-story stone building, angular and somehow harsh-looking against the black woods behind it. The woods rose as a backdrop to the building, then seemed to end abruptly against the sky.

Alan guessed that the tree-covered ridge was part of the miles of cliffs that bordered the Mississippi River in this part of the state.

Sandy followed his gaze. "That's where the caves are that I was telling you about. Down over that ridge. Bootleggers' caves. We can go down there tomorrow if you want."

The truck turned off the road and began bumping across the half-circle hay field toward the stone building. The bumping made it too hard to talk now. Alan had all he could do just to stay standing. Finally the truck slowed, turned, and backed up to the door of the building.

"This doesn't look like a barn to me," said Alan.

He and Sandy waited while Mr. West slipped the bolts in the tailgate and let it down. Then the two jumped to the ground.

"It's not a barn," Mr. West said. He pulled open the double plank doors of the building. "It was an inn, a stagecoach stop, originally. Then it was a house for a long time, and then it started falling apart. It's stood empty for probably twenty or thirty years."

Alan looked up and around with new interest. A stagecoach stop—wow, he thought. Stagecoaches charging up; sweaty, frothy horses; John Wayne riding shotgun. Wow. The gentle Iowa countryside became a movie screen for his imagination.

"Let's get to work here," Mr. West said. He was already carrying out hay bales and dumping them in the back of the truck, where Sandy shoved them into place. Alan began carrying bales, too, but he kept looking around as he worked.

The inn was made of huge blocks of limestone, pale tan stones that looked as though they would stand forever. The walls were three feet thick. Weathered gray planks made the shutters and the front door. He couldn't tell much about the inside because hay bales were stacked almost to the rough board ceiling. It looked to him like two big rooms downstairs, but there seemed to be no way to the second floor.

"It's not very big for an inn," he said to Sandy, who was working beside him now.

She gave him a wry look. "What did you expect—the McGregor Hilton? It was built a hundred years ago, maybe more than that. This is the way inns were back then."

Alan climbed to the top of a stairstep stack and began pulling bales down to where Mr. West could reach them. As he pulled one away from the wall, a door frame and the top few inches of a door came into view.

"Where does this door go?" he asked.

Sandy climbed up beside him. "Beats me."

"You mean you never explored in here before? Here's this neat old place right on your own farm, and you never explored it?"

"It's not on our farm," she snapped. "My dad just started renting this place last year, and he's been storing extra hay in it most of the time. I've looked around in it some, but I just never thought it was all that interesting. I like the caves better. And besides, the horses keep me pretty busy."

Alan couldn't decide whether Sandy deliberately rubbed it in sometimes, about her family's horses, or whether his own envy made it seem that way. He said in a somewhat huffy voice, "Well, I don't know about you, but I'd sure like to see where this door goes."

Outside, Mr. West slammed up the tailgate on the full load of hay. "Come on, you kids. Let's go."

Sandy looked from Alan to the enticing bit of door that showed behind the stack where they were sitting. "I think we'll stay here awhile and walk home, okay?" she called.

"Not too late, or you'll miss supper."

"I never miss a meal," she laughed.

"Okay, then." The pickup door slammed, and in a roar man and truck were gone.

A heavy stillness settled on the place. For the first time Alan became aware of a feeling in the air. It was as though all the old loves and hatreds and fears of all the people who had lived within these walls were floating in the air with the dust motes. The sun was almost down, and the shadows that striped the room were long and deep and cold.

Alan and Sandy went to work, hard and fast, shifting hay bales away from the door. When they got down to the latch, they tried it, but the door was made to open toward them. They had to move all of the bales before they could pull it open.

Behind the door lay a stairway, the narrowest and steepest that Alan had ever seen. He climbed it, with Sandy close be-hind. Upstairs, the space was divided down the middle into two long, narrow rooms tucked under the eaves. There was no fur-niture, only dust and the smell of bats and mice.

"How could it be an inn without more rooms than this?" Alan wondered out loud.

Sandy said, "I think the men slept on one side and the women on the other, just in rows of beds."

Alan laughed. "Huh. Wonder how much the people who stayed here had to pay for all this luxury."

Opposite the head of the stairs was a small window. Alan went to it and rubbed away the grime with his jacket sleeve. Sandy rubbed herself a clean place next to his, and they peered out.

They were looking down at the edge of the woods behind the inn. The last golden-pink light from the setting sun struck the tree trunks, making the woods beyond seem even darker in contrast.

Suddenly a figure appeared against the black-green forest—a man, in a uniform that was out of place and yet strangely familiar. He stood defiantly, arms crossed, head high.

He looked up at the window—and he laughed.

His laughter echoed around Alan and Sandy. It had an unearthly quality, and yet it seemed to spring from enjoyment of a huge and very real joke.

Alan and Sandy turned, together, and fled down the stairs, out of the building, away.

Chapter 2

Mr. West was throwing hay bales from the truck into a barn lot full of horses when Alan and Sandy arrived, breathless from their run.

"Daddy," Sandy said, "we saw a man, out behind the hay barn. And he was wearing a kind of funny uniform."

Mr. West stopped working and turned his attention to his daughter. "What kind of uniform? What was he doing?"

"Just standing there. Laughing," Sandy said.

Alan suddenly realized why the uniform had seemed familiar. "It was like a Civil War uniform," he said.

Mr. West frowned as though he didn't

believe a word of it, but he motioned them into the truck and jumped in himself. "We'll go take a look. I don't much like the idea of tramps hanging around my hay barn. Too much danger of them starting a fire."

They drove back to the stone inn. It was nearly dark now, but in the sunset's pink afterglow Alan saw something he hadn't noticed before. The beam over the front door was carved with the words "Great River Inn." The sign set his imagination into action again. Suddenly, here in this place, a man in a Civil War uniform seemed more believable to Alan than twentieth-century people in a GM pickup truck.

They got out of the truck and walked around to the back of the building. There was no one in sight.

"Hello," Mr. West bellowed. "Anyone out here?"

The woods gave back silence.

Alan said, "He was standing right there, Mr. West, beside that pine tree. I remember clearly."

Snow lay on the ground, old snow, compacted by the March melting to just a few inches of depth. It showed rabbit tracks,

raccoon tracks, the dainty cloven prints of a deer.

But no human tracks.

None.

"You kids must have been seeing things," Mr. West said flatly. "There was no one here. Look for yourselves. No footprints anywhere." He turned, disgruntled, and led the way back to the truck.

It was full dark by the time they got back to the farm. Alan helped Sandy and her father finish the evening chores. He stroked the horses' noses and listened to Sandy's explanations of which horse was which. On this gelding Mr. West had won the Northeast Iowa reining class championship last year. This mare was Sandy's sister's gaming horse. And this one would be Sandy's barrel-racing horse in a few years when she was old enough.

At any other time Alan would have been fascinated. Sandy's horses were one of the most interesting things about Sandy, and one of the biggest reasons Alan had wanted to spend the weekend at her house was the hope of getting to ride.

But now he couldn't pull his mind away from that soldier. That laughing soldier, in a uniform from the Civil War. That figure

who left no footprints in the snow.

He *had* been there. Alan was sure of that. Alan had seen the figure clearly, and so had Sandy. They had heard the laughter.

Could two people imagine the same thing? Alan asked himself. Not likely. So then, who had been out there? Who was that soldier?

At last the chores were finished. Alan was stiff-fingered with the cold and painfully hungry. The warmth and fragrance of the farmhouse kitchen smothered him deliciously. They sat down at the long table in the kitchen—Alan and Sandy, Mr. and Mrs. West, and Sandy's older brother and sister, Todd and Nancy, who mostly ignored Sandy and her guest. That was fine with Alan. His mind was busy with the puzzle of the laughing soldier.

"What took you so long?" Mrs. West asked her husband, when the meal was blessed and begun.

"Oh," he said, piling potatoes on his plate, "the kids thought they saw somebody hanging around over at the stone barn. Some man. Thought we'd better go have a look around. But it was just their imaginations."

"No, it wasn't," Sandy insisted. "We both

saw him. He was a Civil War soldier."

Todd and Nancy exploded in hoots.

"A Civil War soldier?" Todd smirked. "Ol' Sandy's finally gone bonkers. Too much homework. The child's got brain fever."

He and Nancy roared and poked at each other.

"That's enough," their mother warned.

The older two settled into quiet gibes and Sandy turned stubbornly to her plate.

Alan said, "Mr. West was telling us that the stone barn used to be a stagecoach stop. Was it really?"

"So the story goes," Mrs. West said. "Here, start the butter and pass it, would you? Yes, it's quite an old building. A pretty place, I've always thought. If the roof wasn't so far gone, it could be made into a nice house."

Alan took some butter, awkwardly, and passed it. "Was it a stagecoach stop during the Civil War?"

Mrs. West looked up thoughtfully, pondering dates. "Yes, it must have been. It was built in the 1830s some time, and I think it was used as an inn up till, oh, the early 1900s. Wasn't there some sort of story . . ." She scowled, trying to remember.

"Something about some money that was

lost there," Todd said. "Mr. Dingman was talking about it one time. What the heck did he say? I can't remember now. Something about—"

Nancy interrupted. "It wasn't about lost money, dimwit. It was about a guy who got poisoned. Or was it stabbed? Anyhow, something like that."

"Who? When?" Alan stopped eating. The laughing soldier filled his head. The laughter rang in his ears. He felt close to something important, something astonishing.

"Beats me." Nancy shrugged and went back to her eating. Todd shook his head as though trying to remember, but he added nothing to the information Alan needed.

"Who is Mr. Dingman?" Alan asked, reaching for any kind of lead.

Mrs. West said, "He owns the property. We just rent the hay field from him, because we don't have quite enough hay land to feed the horses through the winter. And Mr. Dingman lets us store our extra hay in the old inn building. That's all it's good for anymore."

Alan ate in silence. The Wests had no more answers to his questions. But the questions obsessed him, and he knew he would go back to the inn. He had to.

Chapter 3

It seemed to Alan that Sandy was never going to be finished with her Saturday morning chores.

"This is the price you pay," she puffed, "for having twenty horses to ride."

They were cleaning the stalls in the main barn. Sandy had told Alan he didn't have to help, but he wanted to. He was eager to get back to the inn, and helping Sandy through her work seemed the fastest way to get there.

They shoveled manure from the stalls into a huge, heavy wheelbarrow and carted it away. Then they filled the wheelbarrow with load after load of sawdust from a sawdust mountain behind the barn and spread it, inches deep, in each of the stalls.

When they were done at last, Sandy took a pair of saddlebags from the tack room and ran to the house. She came back with the leather pouches bulging.

"Peanut butter and jelly sandwiches, sugar cookies, and a thermos of hot chocolate," she said, grinning. "Now we won't have to come home till suppertime."

They saddled Sandy's bay mare and a fat blue-eyed pinto for Alan. Then they were off. It was a gray day. The air was cold and wet, and the sky seemed to hang heavy, just above the trees. Alan's feet and fingers were already numb with cold. He wasn't at all sure he wanted to be out in this weather all day, but he didn't dare say so. Sandy had never called him a town kid, but he felt she might very well be thinking it.

As they rode out the farm lane, Sandy said, "I can hardly wait to show you the caves. Bootleggers used to use them as a place to hide their whiskey. See, Iowa used to be a dry state. That meant selling liquor was illegal here. But it wasn't illegal in Wisconsin, and Wisconsin is just across the

river. So these guys—they were crooks was what they were—they'd buy whiskey in Wisconsin, bring it across in their boats on dark nights, and hide it in these caves along the river. And then they'd sell it to other crooks and make a bunch of money."

By this time they had reached the road. Sandy reined her horse to the right, but Alan held back.

"Let's go over to the inn first," he said. "I'd like to take another look around there. Just for the heck of it. Okay?"

He was aware that, since supper last night, Sandy had said nothing about the soldier they had seen. Because she seemed to be avoiding the subject, Alan hadn't mentioned it either, until now.

He could tell from the look on her face that Sandy didn't really want to go back to the inn. But she said, "I guess we could, just for a little while. Then I'll show you the bootleggers' caves, okay?"

When they got to the inn, they tied their horses to a low-hanging tree branch and walked around the building. At the rear corner Sandy hung back just a bit, but then she caught up. Together, they stared at the spot beside the pine tree where they had seen the soldier.

Today the woods were still and empty. Alan and Sandy, in unison, sighed with relief. It was as though they had looked a fear in the face and conquered it.

Feeling suddenly brave, Alan said, "Let's look around inside some more."

They turned and went into the inn through a half-fallen back door. They climbed over pyramids of hay bales, went upstairs, and looked more closely at the two long bedrooms. Flushed with their own bravery, they ran back downstairs and outside, loosened the horses' cinches so they could rest more comfortably, then took the saddlebags from Sandy's mare.

Lunch was served in the dining room of the Great River Inn—peanut butter and jelly sandwiches, sugar cookies, and hot chocolate on a bale of hay. Alan and Sandy joked about the meal. It was almost comfortably warm inside the thick-walled old building.

Alan leaned against a prickly hay bale. He was full and contented and a little sleepy. He wasn't used to spending so much time outdoors in cold weather. He watched Sandy close up the thermos, lick the last bit of chocolate off the cap, and stuff thermos and sandwich wrappers back into the saddlebags.

"You didn't want to come here this morning, did you?" he said.

She gave him a straight look. "Not much."

"Because of—what we saw yesterday? The soldier?"

"In a way."

He waited for her to go on, and after a while she did.

"The thing is, I've seen him before."

Alan sat up straight. He opened his mouth, but Sandy went on, talking faster now.

"It was a long time ago. I never told anybody about it because I wasn't supposed to go this far away from home by myself. I was just little then. But I'd seen this old building from the road, and I wanted to explore it. That was before we were renting the land. So I snuck off one day when my mom was having a club meeting at the house and wasn't paying much attention to me."

"What happened?"

"Well, I couldn't get inside. They kept the door locked then. I think there was some furniture stored in here or something. But I looked in through the window. That one." She pointed to a side window.

"What did you see?" Alan prompted her impatiently.

"A man. The same one we saw yesterday, in that uniform. He was standing, oh, over about there." She waved one hand toward the center of the room. "He was looking right at me, and he had his hands up around his throat, as though he was choking. His eyes were great big, and his tongue was kind of sticking out, and . . ." She shuddered and looked away.

"And what? What happened?"

"Nothing. He was just there, staring at me with that awful look. I turned and ran as if my tail was on fire. And I never told anybody about him till now. See, I thought he was a tramp or something. Mom is always telling us to keep away from strangers. Not that we ever see any around here. But I figured she'd whale the tar out of me if she found out I'd come all the way over here, alone, and seen a man through the window. I mean, she'd be so scared, thinking about what might have happened to me."

Alan pondered. "But you're sure it was the same man?"

Sandy nodded.

"Then you know he must be a . . ." Alan

hesitated, not wanting to say what was in his mind. "He must be a ghost."

Sandy laughed nervously. "Why do you say that? Why couldn't he just be a tramp who likes it here?"

Alan shook his head. "If a tramp was living here, year after year, there'd be signs of him. Cooking stuff, blankets, something. And your dad would have seen him probably. No, I think he's a ghost, and I think he has something to do with that story Todd and Nancy were talking about last night—about somebody getting killed, or some lost money, or whatever."

"Do you believe in ghosts?" Sandy asked abruptly.

"I don't know. Do you?"

"I don't know either."

"Could we go talk to that Mr.—what was his name?—who owns this place? Maybe he could tell us about the guy that got killed or robbed or whatever. That might give us some clues, anyhow, about our—ghost, or whatever he is."

"I guess we could. He lives about three miles away, but we could ride there." Sandy and Alan rose and picked up the saddle-bags. "Oh, it's starting to snow," Sandy said as they pushed open the plank door.

The sky had lowered and darkened. The air was full of large, heavy, wet flakes. Alan and Sandy looked at the sky, then at each other.

"I'm game if you are," Alan said.

"Okay. Let's get going, though. That looks like a big old March snowstorm about to dump on us."

They tightened their cinches, untied the horses, and climbed on. The snow on his saddle soaked unpleasantly through Alan's jeans. For an instant he longed to be in the bright, dry warmth of Sandy's house, spending Saturday watching television.

But he set his face into the wind and squinted his eyes against the driving snow. It was going to be a long, cold ride. But maybe, at the end of it, they would find some answers.

Chapter 4

It was indeed a long, cold ride. Alan had no idea three miles could be so long. They followed a gravel road that was fast disappearing under white. Occasionally a car or a pickup truck went by, slowed, then speeded up again after the driver had stared at them. Alan could almost feel the drivers thinking, crazy kids, out riding on a day like this.

"How come Mr. Dingman lives so far away?" Alan asked. It was hard to talk with a cold, stiff face. "I mean, if he owns that land where the inn is?"

Sandy, riding in front, turned and called back, "He owns two or three farms around

here. He lives on the main place, but he's got other property. I think my dad said he inherited the farm where the inn is from his wife's folks. Or something like that."

"Oh."

They rode on in silence.

Three miles just can't be this long, Alan thought. And there's going to be an equally long ride home. And Mr. Dingman might not even be there when we get to his place. This is a dumb idea, he finally admitted. But only to himself.

He was almost ready to surrender his pride and suggest that they turn around, when Sandy said, "That's the Dingmans' place."

It was a new-looking brick house, sitting close to the road. The barns and outbuildings looked unusually well cared for. As they rode in, an overalled figure came toward them from the barns.

"Mr. Dingman," Sandy said under her breath to Alan.

The man came close. He didn't quite smile, but his face looked friendly, Alan thought.

"Sandy West, isn't it? What the dickens are you kids doing so far from home in this weather? Did you get lost?"

"No, we came on purpose. I don't get lost," Sandy said with heavy dignity. "This is my friend Alan, and we wanted to ask you about that old building on my dad's hay field. The one that used to be a stage-coach inn."

"Well, for Pete's sake," Mr. Dingman said, "no need you two sitting out here like a couple of icicles. We'll put your horses in the barn, let them thaw out, too. Then we'll go up to the house and talk where we can be comfortable."

The Dingmans' living room was bright-ened by a fire in a modern brick fireplace. Alan backed up to the warmth of it and hugged himself in relief. With pricks of pain, the feeling began coming back in his feet and hands and forehead.

Mrs. Dingman fussed over them, taking their wet jackets, pulling chairs close to the fire for them. "I'll fix you some coffee," she said. "Oh, no. You're probably too young for coffee. Tea? Hot chocolate? How about a mug of hot tomato soup? That's it." She disappeared into the kitchen.

When Mr. Dingman was settled deep in the big brown chair that was obviously his,

and Sandy and Alan were hunched near the fire, Mr. Dingman said, "Okay now. Shoot."

Sandy began. "We were talking at supper last night about the old inn, back when that's what it was. Todd and Nancy were trying to tell us some story or other, but they had it all confused, and we were curious."

Alan nodded. "It was something about somebody getting killed, and some lost money. It was in Civil War time, I think."

"Oh, sure," Mr. Dingman said. "I know what they were talking about. That was Captain . . ." He paused, trying to remember the name.

From the kitchen Mrs. Dingman called, "Greer."

"That's it. Captain Greer. The name slipped my mind for a minute. I was telling about him, somewhere or other, a while back. I think it was at the Farm Bureau, or was it at the church potluck? Do you remember, Margaret?"

"It doesn't matter where you were telling it. These children rode all the way over here in a snowstorm; they want to hear the story, not your social life." Mrs. Dingman brought mugs of steaming soup to Sandy and Alan.

"Sandy, shall I call your mom and let her know you're here, in case she's worrying?"

"Yes, thanks," Sandy said.

Mr. Dingman raised his voice as his wife disappeared again. "Hon, tell her I'll run the kids home in a little bit, so they won't have to ride back. I've got the stock truck out anyhow, so it won't be any trouble to drive them and the horses home."

Alan melted into the pleasure of knowing they wouldn't have to ride all that long way home in the cold. He said, "Thanks, Mr. Dingman. That would be awful nice. Now, you started to say about Captain—"

"Greer. Yes. It was my wife's grandad who first told me about what happened at the inn. I wasn't much more than your age at the time. Margaret and I were great buddies, even back then when we were children. I used to spend about as much time at her place as I did at home. Her grandad lived with them, and the old gentleman took a liking to me, and me to him."

Alan tried not to look impatient.

Mr. Dingman went on. "The old man was born and raised on that farm. It'd been in his family since this area was first settled. It was an uncle of his who ran the inn. There were lots of stories about the old place. Stories get handed down in a family, just like property. But this was the one I liked best, and the old man told it to me more than once."

Mr. Dingman settled deeper in his chair, and his story began.

Chapter 5

It was late on a snowy evening in March 1863 when Captain Jacob Greer, Union Army Paymaster Corps, dismounted outside the Great River Inn. He handed over his horse to a waiting boy, with orders for a double measure of grain for the animal. If his fears proved out, he thought, he might be in need of a well-fed horse on which to get away.

He walked into the welcoming brightness and warmth of the inn. Although he was bone weary from hours in the saddle, he carried himself with unusual tension. He knew it and tried to relax, tried to act normal, like an ordinary traveler stopping for the night.

But the money belt made itself felt around his waist. It bulged with bills—twenty thousand dollars. Captain Greer was carrying three months' pay for the soldiers at Fort Crawford, twelve miles away in Wisconsin. This was the last stopover on the hazardous journey from his headquarters in Fort Dodge. Every three months for the past year he had made this trip, and others like it, to various army camps. Four times he had been beaten and robbed by other travelers who knew, or sensed, that he carried a huge sum of money.

He paid the innkeeper for his night's lodging. It would be a straw mattress on the floor of a dormitory room, he knew. He'd stayed here before. It would be no better and no worse than most places along the way, but it would offer little sleep for Jacob Greer—not with twenty thousand dollars around his waist, not with hard-eyed strangers sleeping all around him, or pretending to sleep.

"You'll be wanting supper, Captain?" the innkeeper said. "Got some beef stew left."

Suddenly weary beyond bearing, Greer nodded and sank onto the end of the long bench that held his fellow diners. Half a dozen men and two women sat at the long

plank table that filled most of the inn's main room. One of the men got up and went into the kitchen beyond the stairway. In a few minutes he came back with a bowl of beef stew, which he set before Captain Greer.

"Here you go, mate," the man said. "Cook's a little busy back there. Thought I'd lend a hand. You look as though you need a pick-me-up. Here, drink this down and see if it doesn't revive you some." He set a mug of beer beside Greer's plate.

"Thanks. I could do with some of that," Greer said. He drained off half the mug in one draw, then began eating his stew. Here, in this room full of people, he felt momentarily safe. The danger would come later, upstairs in the dark.

But before he was halfway through the steaming bowl of stew, he knew, horribly, that he'd been wrong. Intense pain gripped his stomach and made his face go white.

"I've been poisoned!" He staggered to his feet, clutching his throat, and ran unsteadily toward the door. I've got to get out of here, he thought wildly. Got to get away.

Mr. Dingman paused.
"What happened?" Sandy demanded.

"Nobody knows for sure. He ran out the door. It took the other people in the room maybe half a minute to get their wits about them. Then they ran out after him. Found him just a little ways off from the inn, face down in the snow. Deader than a codfish. And"—he paused for drama—"the money belt wasn't on him."

"Somebody must have taken it," Alan said, "before the others got out there. You said it took them a little time."

Mr. Dingman shook his head. "The fellow was lying in fresh snow. Not a sign of a track around him. If anybody'd robbed him, they'd have had to leave footprints. And besides, there was hardly time to have gotten the money belt unbuckled and off the body."

Sandy and Alan both shivered.

"Then what happened to the money belt?" Alan persisted.

Mr. Dingman shook his head. "It never was found. Some people figured he'd found a hiding place for it, just before he died. People have turned that place upside down looking for it. Never found a trace."

Chapter 6

"That money belt had to go somewhere. It didn't just disappear," Alan insisted.

He and Sandy stood in front of the inn door, squinting out across the hay field. It was a dazzling gold and white morning. Even the air sparkled. The sound of Sunday morning church bells came clearly from two miles away.

"You know this is crazy, don't you?" Sandy said. "It all happened more than a hundred years ago. That land out there has been plowed I don't know how many times. If Captain Greer had hid the money belt anyplace between here and where he died, someone would have found it long before now."

"I know that. But still . . ." He didn't finish. His mind was busy with the puzzle. Several times this morning he had gone through the motions of the soldier. He sat in the inn on a hay bale. He stood up, clutching his throat; he ran outside, staggering, unbuckling his belt as he ran, weaving, falling, groaning his last. Each time he ran in a slightly different direction. Each time he looked for some place, any place, where he could hide his belt.

By now the snow in front of the inn was well stirred by his feet and by the horses' hoofprints, made when they rode in.

"That's what's wrong!" Alan shouted. "He couldn't have come out this door. Mr. Dingman said there weren't any tracks around where Greer fell and died. If he'd come out the front door, this whole area would have been tracked up, from travelers and horses and all that. It must have been the back door he ran out."

Sandy caught his excitement. "Sure. We should have thought of it before. That's where we saw the . . ."

Their eyes met. They still didn't like using the word "ghost" when they talked about what they had seen. They avoided saying it, but the thought was there.

"Come on."

They ran to the back of the building and began to search.

"How can we find anything in this snow?" Sandy muttered.

"Don't forget it was snowing that night when Captain Greer died, too."

They searched for more than two hours, scuffling through the snow, stirring the dead leaves beneath it. Alan grew more and more discouraged.

This is stupid, he finally admitted to himself. We aren't going to find anything. Not more than a hundred years after the murder. Not two kids, kicking through the snow.

"Come on," Sandy said. "We're wasting the whole day. Let's get the horses and ride up along the ridge." She motioned to the upward slope of the woods behind them. "We can follow the cliff back south a ways to my caves. Okay?"

"Sure." Alan knew she was eager to show off her caves. In a few hours his mother would be coming to pick him up, and the weekend would be over. He hated to give up the search, but he knew Sandy was right. They couldn't possibly find that money belt, and they were wasting precious time.

They got the horses from their hitching tree in front of the inn. Alan winced as he climbed up onto the pinto. He was painfully stiff from yesterday's long ride. He reined in behind Sandy, then followed her horse around the building and into the woods.

"I think we can short-cut up through here," Sandy said. "I've never ridden back here, but it looks like a deer path up there a ways."

Alan opened his mouth to answer, but suddenly the front end of his horse dropped to the ground. Alan somersaulted and landed on the ground, on his back . He was already scrambling to his feet, startled but unhurt, when Sandy turned and came back.

"Are you all right?"

"Sure," he said. "I guess Arrow tripped or something." The horse was standing, head high and eyes rolling, but otherwise all right.

Alan looked at the ground. "I wonder what he could have—oh, look. There it is. That hole. He must have stepped in it."

The hole was just the size and shape of

Arrow's hoof, as though the hoof had created the hole. "Isn't that funny?" Alan murmured. He put his hand in the hole to feel its depth.

There was no bottom.

"Hey, is this ever deep, Sandy. Look. Come here."

She knelt beside him and thrust her entire arm into the hole. "I can't feel the bottom, and there aren't any sides, even." She brushed away the snow and dead leaves from around the hole.

The bared earth revealed a crack about two feet long. Except for where Arrow's hoof had broken through, it was hardly more than an inch wide.

Alan bent double, closed one eye, and squinted down into the hole, expecting to see nothing.

But he saw light. Far below and faint, but there it was—daylight, deep within the earth.

Chapter 7

From the rim of the cliff Alan looked at the Mississippi River stretching away into the distance below. The river was black in the main channel where the barges were already breaking ice, and blue-white closer to shore where snow-covered ice sheathed the water.

In front of Alan and Sandy the land dropped off abruptly. Jagged boulders of pale cream stone littered the cliffside. Blue-green cedars and white-barked birch trees grew out of the almost vertical slope.

"Do you think we can climb down there?" Alan asked with doubt in his voice.

"Oh, sure. I've done it lots of times. Not

here. South a ways, on our own farm. But this is no steeper. There's got to be a cave down here. That has to be where that light is coming from. And we're not going to find it by standing around up here."

Alan looked back. The inn was not far behind them, straight through the narrow belt of woods. He tried to memorize the distance from the cliff edge to the crack in the ground. Then he began a sliding descent, behind Sandy.

Going down was easy. They half-slid, half-walked from tree to boulder to tree, catching themselves as they went. They hadn't gone far when they saw it.

It was a giant crack in the rock face of the cliff, an upright crack, big enough to walk into. In summer it would be hidden by the sumac bushes growing around it, but this morning, with the bushes winter-bare and the sun striking full on the east-facing cliff, the cave opening was as clear as ink on paper.

Sandy stood aside and allowed Alan to go in first. Just beyond the opening the cave widened so that they could stand comfortably and walk side by side. They entered a long, narrow chamber that reached up nearly to ground level. It seemed to Alan more like a huge crack in the rock structure of the cliff than an actual cave.

He looked up at the high ceiling and saw two or three tiny cracks of daylight. He pointed them out to Sandy. "Looks like a few places where the ground sort of broke through. I'll bet you anything we're going to find that money belt in here."

Sandy's voice reflected his own excitement. "Sure. You wouldn't see those narrow little cracks in the ground from above. Not unless you had fallen and were lying face down right on top of one of them. And I'll bet that's just what Captain Greer did."

They walked on, more slowly as the light dimmed.

"I sure wish I had a flashlight," Sandy muttered.

Alan wrinkled his nose. "It sure stinks in here."

"That's bats. The place is probably full of them."

"Oh, thanks for telling me."

"Bats won't hurt you, unless they have rabies. Then they'll bite you and you'll die. But they sleep in the daytime, so they probably won't bother us."

Alan walked on, uncomforted.

The cave grew narrow. They had to walk single file.

"We should be almost there," Alan whispered. He didn't want to wake any sleeping bats.

Suddenly he stopped. Just before him a beam of light shone down from a narrow crack overhead, a crack with a hoof-sized wide spot.

Holding his breath, Alan looked down. At first he saw nothing where the daylight pointed, nothing but an accumulation of earth and leaf bits that had sifted down through the years from the crack above.

Then he saw it, lying just to the side of the light beam, as though it had bounced after striking the cave floor. It was green with age and mold, but there it was—Captain Greer's money belt.

Alan picked it up, gently, and held it under the beam of light where Sandy could see, too. It was a broad heavy-buckled belt made of thick leather. All along the inner surface of the belt was a series of pouches.

Alan's heart pounded as he lifted the flap on one pouch and looked inside.

The paper money had crumbled almost to powder, and on top of the soft bed of money dust was a nest of baby mice!

Suddenly Alan began to laugh. All those people, searching all those years, for a lost fortune, and here it was, keeping a family of mice warm. Sandy stared at him and began to laugh, too.

And the air about them carried the echo of another laugh, the soldier's laugh, rich and deep and only slightly bitter.

AUTHOR'S NOTE

Although Alan and Sandy and the ghost are fictitious,
this story is based on an actual happening. The captain,
the inn, the poisoning, the payroll money lost for a hundred
years, all of these were real.

Lynn Hall

About the Author

Lynn Hall has written more than twenty-five books for young readers. Because she has always loved dogs and horses and they fill a big portion of her life, many of her books are about them. Even when she is not specifically writing about dogs or horses, these favorite animals often sneak into her stories and play at least minor roles.

In recent years Ms. Hall has realized a lifelong dream with the completion of Touchwood, a small stone cottage planted squarely in the middle of twenty-five acres of woods and hills in northeast Iowa. "I designed the house myself," she writes, "and have had a hand in all phases of its construction, doing all but the heavy work myself, so it is a home in all the best senses of the word."

At Touchwood Ms. Hall also has built a kennel and small stable. There she raises English cocker spaniels and Paso Fino horses, which she breeds and shows in competition throughout the country.